Hello, Day!

Anita Lobel

Greenwillow Books
An Imprint of HarperCollinsPublishers

The sun rose.
Good morning.

The Rooster said,

"Cock-a-doodle-doo!"

The Cow said, "Moo."

The Sheep said,

"Baa."

The Horse said, "Neigh."

The Dog said,
"Woof."

The Cat said, "Meow."

The Mouse said,

"Eeeek."

The Rabbit said,

"Pr-pr-pr."

The Goose said,

"Honk."

The Pig said, "Oink."

What they all meant was

"Hello, day!"

The sun set.
The moon rose.

The Owl said,

"Whoo-ooo."

What she meant was . . .

"Good night!"

For Billy, who named it;
Virginia, who gave me the idea;
and Paul, who rescued it.
With love, A. L.

Markers, pencil, colored pencil, watercolors, and gouache
were used to prepare the full-color art.
The text type is Geometric 415 and AntiqueOpti-Fourteen.

Library of Congress Cataloging-in-Publication Data
Lobel, Anita.
Hello, day! / by Anita Lobel.
p. cm.
"Greenwillow Books."
Summary: Various animals greet the sunrise in their own unique voices,
except for the owl who welcomes the night.
ISBN-13: 978-0-06-078765-3 (trade bdg.) ISBN-10: 0-06-078765-1 (trade bdg.)
ISBN-13: 978-0-06-078766-0 (lib. bdg.) ISBN-10: 0-06-078766-X (lib. bdg.)
[1. Sun—Rising and setting—Fiction. 2. Morning—Fiction.
3. Animals—Fiction. 4. Animal sounds—Fiction.] I. Title.
PZ7.L7794He 2008 [E]—dc22 2007018361

First Edition 10 9 8 7 6 5 4 3 2 1

 Greenwillow Books